Disney's Me and my Dad

MOUSE WORKS

One day me and my dad went to the beach. I wanted to bring fins and snorkels and surfboards. "If you make a list you won't forget anything, Max," my dad said. But, I didn't need a list, because I am very good at remembering.

I loaded up the
car with everything —
towels and umbrellas and beach
chairs and masks. Everything!

Just as soon as we got on the highway
I heard thump-it, thump-it, thump-it.
It was not a good sound.

My dad said I shouldn't
worry. It was only a flat tire.

"What do we do now?" I asked. I was worried because I'd taken out the spare tire and all that junk to make room for the important beach stuff. "No problem, Maxie," laughed my dad.

"We just change the tire. Luckily, I put back
the things we will need before we left home!"

So Dad jacked up the car. It was a good thing I was there, because the car started to roll. "Dad!" I hollered. "You should put some rocks under the tires, right?" Was he ever glad I saw that!

I got a big rock and put it under the back tire. He said, "Thanks, Max. You're a great helper. Now, help me tighten these lug nuts and then we're off!"

It didn't take long after that to get to the beach.
We unloaded all the stuff and set up the umbrellas,
beach chairs and towels.

My dad said, "Hand me the suntan lotion, Maxie."
That's when I remembered that I'd forgotten to bring
any. "You were right about that list, Dad," I said.

"Don't worry, son," said my dad. "We'll just buy some before we go in the water." So me and my dad went to the little food stand. We got a few extra things to eat, too.

It was lucky that I went with him, because
he forgot his money. Even dads forget!

Then me and my dad put on our masks and went snorkeling.
We saw all kinds of fish and shells and seaweed.

I told Dad the names of everything. I know all that stuff because I learned it in school. "Look at this little fellow," said my dad. It was the cutest little baby seahorse!

Later we found a tide pool full of fish and things. My dad put some clams in the bucket.

I picked up a shell that was walking on the sand. Me and
my dad laughed at the funny little hermit crab living inside.
When we looked for more shell houses, we found a bunch.

Soon I got cold and hungry, too. Me and my dad had lunch. "It's a good thing you brought all this food," I told him. "Being at the beach makes a guy really hungry."

"Being at the beach makes a guy really sleepy, too," said my dad. I wasn't sleepy. But I decided to let him rest because parents get tired easily.

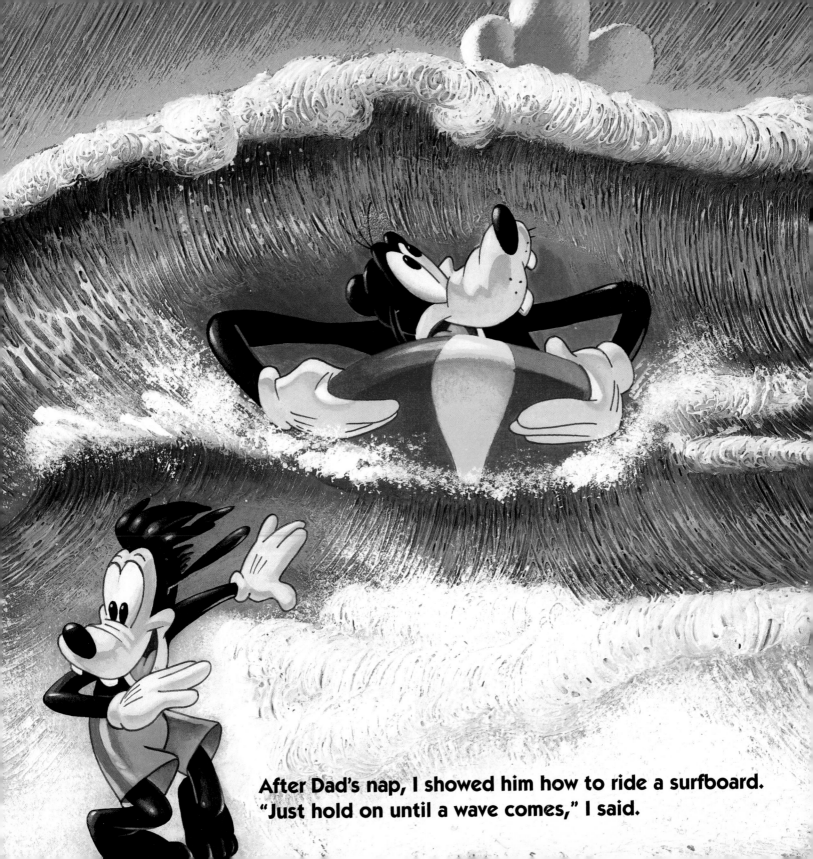

After Dad's nap, I showed him how to ride a surfboard.
"Just hold on until a wave comes," I said.

"Then kick and paddle as hard as you can."
Pretty soon a big wave came. I jumped on my
board and yelled, "Go now, Dad!"

After I'd given Dad lots of lessons,
he started to get the hang of it. "Wow!
This is great, Max," he called out as he caught
his second wave. "Way to go, Dad!" I hollered back.
"You sure are good at this!"

Me and my dad built a sand castle. I bet it was the biggest sand castle the world has ever seen. The trouble was the tide came in! Me and my dad dug trenches and built walls.

But the waves knocked our castle down anyway.
My dad was really upset. I told him, "It's okay,
Dad. We can always build another one."

At last it was time to go home. "You taught
me a lot today, Maxie — about surfing and
everything. We sure had a great time
together!" said my dad.
And he was right.